Sparkly!

D0543724

In memory of Elizabeth Tamara Angelique Spencer
29 May 2010 – 10 December 2015 ~ T C x

For my nephew Jonah, and all our Christmases to come!
x ~ T W

LITTLE TIGER PRESS LTD,
an imprint of the Little Tiger Group
1 Coda Studios, 189 Munster Road, London SW6 6AW
www.littletiger.co.uk

First published in Great Britain 2017
This edition published 2018
Text copyright © Tracey Corderoy 2017
Illustrations copyright © Tim Warnes 2017
Visit Tim Warnes at www.ChapmanandWarnes.com
Tracey Corderoy and Tim Warnes have asserted their rights to be identified as the author
and illustrator of this work under the Copyright, Designs and Patents Act, 1988
A CIP catalogue record for this book is available from the British Library

ISBN 978-1-84869-672-3
Printed in China • LTP/1400/2188/0518
2 4 6 8 10 9 7 5 3 1

It's Christmas!

Tracey Corderoy

Tim Warnes

dinosaurs
bricks
sledge!
digger
rocket

LITTLE TiGER
LONDON

Christmas was coming
and Archie was excited.
More excited than **EVER!**

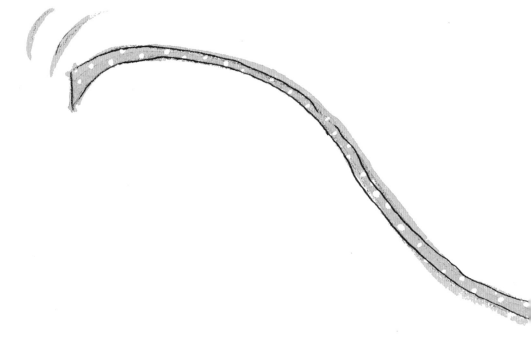

Dad's Christmas biscuits smelled yummy.

But Archie wanted to make them
even better.

So he plopped on more icing and shook on **LOTS** of sprinkles.

"Look, Dad!" said Archie. "Christmas penguins!"

Next Archie helped Mum decorate the tree. But the new decorations weren't quite right . . .

Those aren't **Christmassy** enough!

So Archie found the old ones instead.

Ooo!

Sparkly!

He even found the star
that **NEVER** stopped flashing!
"Now it really feels like Christmas!"
Archie smiled.

Ding-dong! went the doorbell.
It was Granny and Grandpa in their lovely
Christmas jumpers!

Archie looked
down at his
jumper and
sighed.

It's not
Christmassy
enough!

So out came his craft box and Archie got busy . . .

"Ta-daa!" Archie beamed, and he gave a little twirl.

"Mind the tree!" Grandpa cried as it

wibbled and

wobbled

and . . .

"Now then," said Mum, "I wonder . . .
who would like a **VERY** Christmassy job?"

Mum sat Archie down by the window.
"I need you to watch . . . for snow,"
she whispered.

"Yay!" cheered Archie.
"Snow is **SUPER**-Christmassy!"

Archie waited, and **waited**, and **WAITED**.

But the snow didn't come.

Not

one

flake.

"This isn't Christmassy at ALL!"

Even Tiger looked sad.

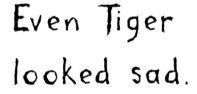

But then Archie had a brilliant idea . . .

"Oh, Archie!" sighed Dad. "Look – you've buried all the presents in the snow!"

So Archie swept the snow off the presents.
But – **OOPS!** – he swept the labels off too!

Where did each one GO?

By Christmas morning everything felt perfectly Christmassy – there was even REAL snow!

"Time to open some presents!" Mum called. They all gathered round. But – **oh dear** – something wasn't quite right.

Dad had Granny's balls of wool,
Mum had Grandpa's fishing rod,
Granny had Dad's drum kit,
and Archie had Mum's
favourite perfume!

Then Grandpa opened the best present of all . . .

Luckily, Mum put everything right.

But Granny loved Dad's drums so much, they let her bang out one more Christmas carol. Now even Archie had to agree . . .

This was the most Christmassy Christmas **EVER!**

The Night Before Christmas
Clement C. Moore
Mark Marshall

One Cosy Christmas
M Christina Butler
Tina Macnaughton

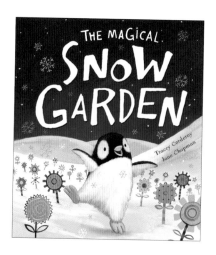

THE MAGICAL SNOW GARDEN
Tracey Corderoy
Jane Chapman

Is It Christmas Yet?
Jane Chapman

LAST STOP ON THE REINDEER EXPRESS

Waiting for Santa
Steve Metzger
Alison Edgson

More Christmassy adventures from Little Tiger Press!

Ooo!

For information regarding any of the above titles
or for our catalogue, please contact us:
Little Tiger Press, 1 Coda Studios,
189 Munster Road, London SW6 6AW
Tel: 020 7385 6333
E-mail: contact@littletiger.co.uk
www.littletiger.co.uk